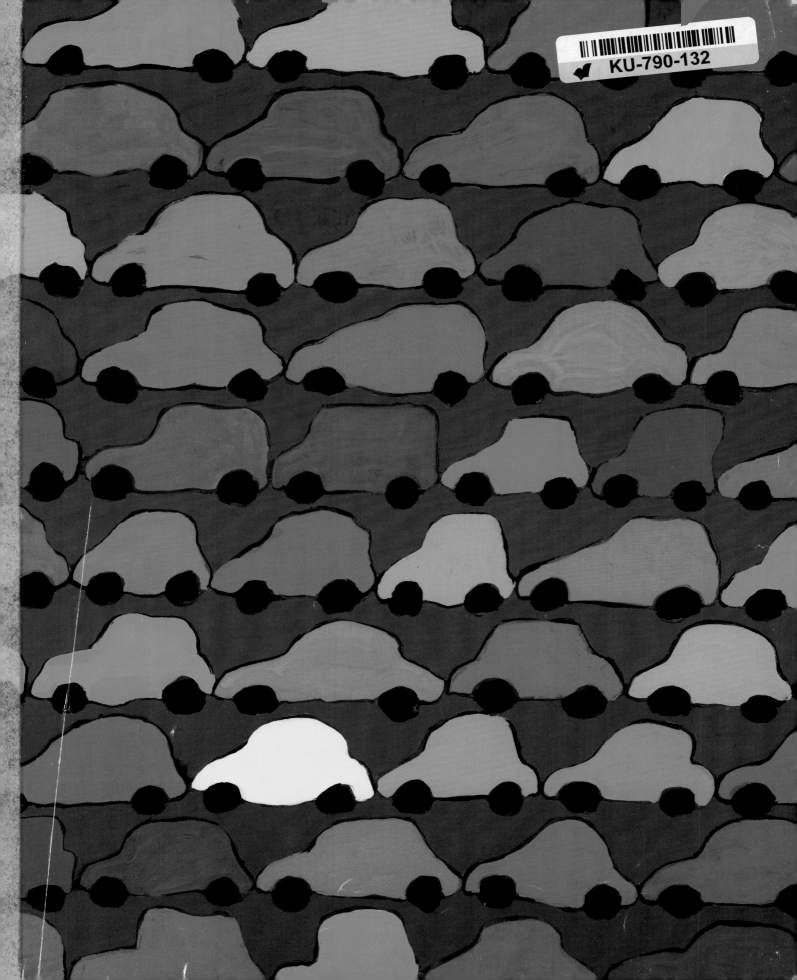

for Luke

Copyright © 1999 by David McKee.
The rights of David McKee to be identified as the author and illustrator
of this work have been asserted by him in accordance with the Copyright,
Designs and Patents Act, 1988.
First published in Great Britain in 1999 by Andersen Press Ltd., 20 Vauxhall Bridge Road,
London SW1V 2SA. Published in Australia by Random House Australia Pty., 20 Alfred Street,
Milsons Point, Sydney, NSW 2061. All rights reserved. Colour separated in Switzerland
by Photolitho AG, Zürich. Printed and bound in Italy by Grafiche AZ, Verona.

10   9   8   7   6   5   4   3   2   1

British Library Cataloguing in Publication Data available.

ISBN 0 86264 909 9

This book has been printed on acid-free paper

MARY'S SECRET

DAVID McKEE

Andersen Press • London

"I need some new shoes," said Mary. "I like to bounce but these shoes don't."

"Oh dear, bouncy shoes are expensive," said Dad.
"Never mind, we'll save up," said Mum.

It was Dad who took Mary to school on his way to work.
It was fun.

They ran, they hid, and they never stepped on the lines.

Mum drove to work in the city. It wasn't fun.

The cars were always bumper to bumper.

One evening, Mum said, "On the way to work today,
I ran out of petrol."
"Oh dear!" said Dad. "What did you do?"

"Nothing," said Mum. "Nobody noticed. The cars were
so close together they pushed me all the way to work."
Dad laughed, "At least you had some fun for a change."

That evening they played a new game – 'cars running out of petrol'. They pushed each other around the room.

Not long after that, Mum bought Mary some very bouncy shoes.

"You saved the money quickly?" said Dad in surprise.
"I saved on petrol," laughed Mum. "Going to work and
coming home I switch off the motor and the others push me."

"That's brilliant, Mum," laughed Mary.
But Dad frowned. "I don't think that's allowed," he said.
"Don't tell anyone. Remember, Mary, it's a secret."

On Monday Mum smiled as she was pushed to work.

At school everyone loved Mary's new shoes.

"Not only that," said Mary. "I've got a secret."
"What is it? What is it?" asked her friends.

"Sorry," said Mary as she bounced away. "A secret is a secret."

Later Mary said to Anne, "You're my best friend, Anne.
I can tell you. But remember, it's a secret."

At lunchtime James and Pamela said, "Come on, Anne.
You're our sister. Tell us Mary's secret." So Anne did.

James, of course, told his friends, Andy, Fred and Lance.

Pamela told Clare and Harriet and Olivia and Zoë.

Then Andy told Brian while Clare told Denise and Emma.
Fred told Gary and Harriet told Ian, John and Kevin.
Lance told Mike and Nicholas.

Olivia told Pamela and Queenie and Richard and Susan and
Tony and Ursula and Victor and Wendy and Xian and Yasmin.
Zoë didn't tell anyone at all. "A secret is a secret," she said.
Besides, everyone already knew.

The next day, at the very worst time, right in the middle
of rush hour, when everyone was on their way to work,

without any warning and to everyone's surprise,
all the traffic came to a sudden, silent, stop.